The 13 Nights of Halloween

by
Rebecca Dickinson

SCHOLASTIC INC.

New York   Toronto   London   Auckland   Sydney

For my three little goblins,
Alisha, Drew, and Aubrey Anne
—R.D.

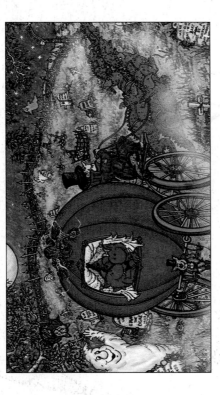

Library of Congress Cataloging-in-Publication Data

Dickinson, Rebecca.
    The 13 nights of Halloween / by Rebecca Dickinson.
        p.   cm.
    Summary: Following the pattern of the folk song, Twelve days of Christmas, a goblin guy gives his goblin gal a different present each of the thirteen nights of Halloween.
        ISBN 0-590-47586-X
    [1. Halloween — Fiction. 2. Twelve days of Christmas (English folk song) — Adaptations. 3. Stories in rhyme.]
    I. Title.
    PZ8.3.D5535Aac 1996
    [E] —dc20
                                                                                            95-30065
                                                                                                CIP
                                                                                                 AC

12 11 10 9 8 7 6 5 4 3 2 1   6 7 8 9/9 0 1/0

                                                    Printed in the U.S.A.

                                            First Scholastic printing, September 1996

Halloween night — as everyone knows —
is when a goblin can propose
to his sweetheart, cute and hairy.
One night to ask her if she will marry.

But once there was a goblin guy
who was rather quiet; a little shy.

"Ah," he sighed, "if I had more time,
I'm sure my true love would be mine.

Oh, to stretch the night and make it longer —
then my courage would grow stronger."

"To capture your true love, your heart's desire,
you need a spell!" said the vampire.

"Yes!" the spiders and lizards chimed,
"Go ask the old witch, she won't mind."

So on the wings of bats he flew,
hoping the witch would know what to do.

Now this dear witch was quite a romantic!
"I'm brewing up potions," she cried. "I'm frantic!"

Then, on that day, she gave him his dream —
with thirteen nights of Halloween!

So here's the tale *Mrs.* Goblin told me
of how her wedding came to be.

—R.D.

Use the pictures on the right-hand pages of this book to follow the goblins' love story; to look for the boldface items in the poem; and to spot this wizard.

On the first night of Halloween,
my goblin gave to me:

A spooky owl
in a gnarled tree.

On the second night of Halloween,
my goblin gave to me:

Two hairy toads,
and a spooky owl
in a gnarled tree.

On the third night of Halloween,
my goblin gave to me:

Three jack-o²-lanterns,

two hairy toads,

and a spooky owl

in a gnarled tree.

On the fourth night of Halloween,
my goblin gave to me:

Four cackling witches,

three jack-o'-lanterns,

two hairy toads,

and a spooky owl

in a gnarled tree.

On the fifth night of Halloween, my goblin gave to me:

Five pounds of worms,

four cackling witches,

three jack-o'-lanterns,

two hairy toads,

and a spooky owl

in a gnarled tree.

On the sixth night of Halloween, my goblin gave to me:

Six spiders spinning,

five pounds of worms,

four cackling witches,

three jack-o'-lanterns,

two hairy toads,

and a spooky owl

in a gnarled tree.

On the seventh night of Halloween, my goblin gave to me:

Seven lizards creeping,
six spiders spinning,
five pounds of worms,
four cackling witches,

three jack-o'-lanterns,
two hairy toads,
and a spooky owl
in a gnarled tree.

**On the eighth night of Halloween,
my goblin gave to me:**

three jack-o'-lanterns,

two hairy toads,

and a spooky owl

in a gnarled tree.

Eight werewolves howling,

seven lizards creeping,

six spiders spinning,

five pounds of worms,

four cackling witches,

**On the ninth night of Halloween,
my goblin gave to me:**

four cackling witches,

three jack-o'-lanterns,

two hairy toads,

and a spooky owl

in a gnarled tree.

Nine bats a-flying,

eight werewolves howling,

seven lizards creeping,

six spiders spinning,

five pounds of worms,

**On the tenth night of Halloween,
my goblin gave to me:**

Ten skeletons rattling,

nine bats a-flying,

eight werewolves howling,

seven lizards creeping,

six spiders spinning,

five pounds of worms,

four cackling witches,

three jack-o'-lanterns,

two hairy toads,

and a spooky owl

in a gnarled tree.

On the eleventh night of Halloween, my goblin gave to me:

Eleven black cats hissing,

ten skeletons rattling,

nine bats a-flying,

eight werewolves howling,

seven lizards creeping,

six spiders spinning,

five pounds of worms,

four cackling witches,

three jack-o'-lanterns,

two hairy toads,

and a spooky owl

in a gnarled tree.

**On the twelfth night of Halloween,
my goblin gave to me:**

Twelve vampires nibbling,

eleven black cats hissing,

ten skeletons rattling,

nine bats a-flying,

eight werewolves howling,

seven lizards creeping,

six spiders spinning,

five pounds of worms,

four cackling witches,

three jack-o'-lanterns,

two hairy toads,

and a spooky owl

in a gnarled tree.

**On the thirteenth night of Halloween,
my goblin gave to me:**

Thirteen ghosts a-booing,

twelve vampires nibbling,

eleven black cats hissing,

ten skeletons rattling,

nine bats a-flying,

eight werewolves howling,

seven lizards creeping,

six spiders spinning,

five pounds of worms,

four cackling witches,

three jack-o'-lanterns,

two hairy toads,

and a spooky owl

in a gnarled tree.

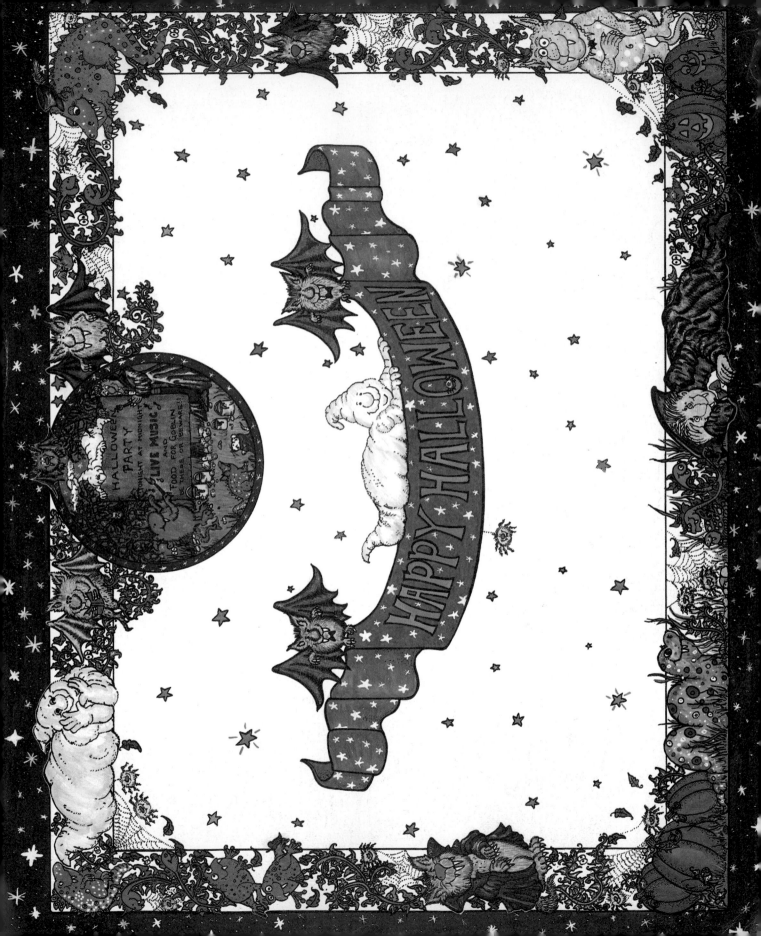

HAPPY HALLOWEEN

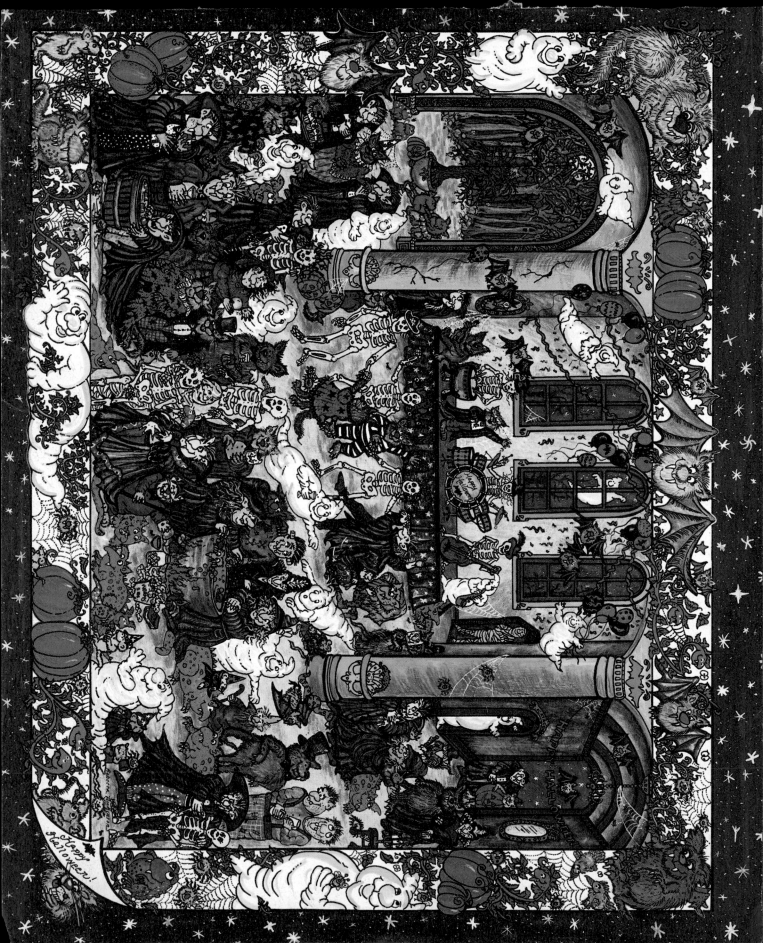

THE END